9/20

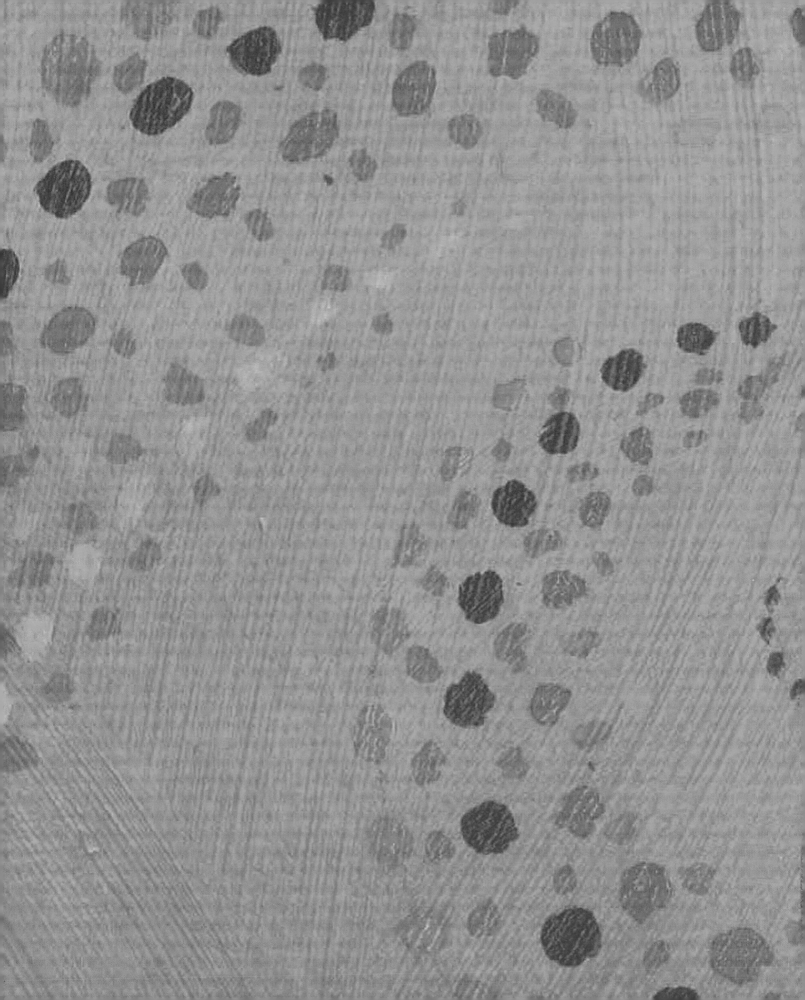

What Can You Do with a Paleta?

by CARMEN TAFOLLA

Illustrated by MAGALY MORALES

TRICYCLE PRESS
BERKELEY · TORONTO

Tricycle Press
an imprint of Ten Speed Press
PO Box 7123
Berkeley, California 94707
www.tricyclepress.com

Design by Katie Jennings
Typeset in Billy and Nanumunga Bold
The illustrations in this book were rendered in acrylic.

Library of Congress Cataloging-in-Publication Data

Tafolla, Carmen, 1951–
What can you do with a paleta? / by Carmen Tafolla ; illustrations by Magaly Morales.
    p. cm.
Summary: A young Mexican American girl celebrates the *paleta*, an icy fruit
popsicle, and the many roles it plays in her lively *barrio*.
ISBN 978-1-58246-221-9 (hardcover : alk. paper)
[1. Ice pops--Fiction. 2. City and town life--Fiction. 3. Mexican
Americans--Fiction.] I. Morales, Magaly, ill. II. Title.
PZ7.T1165Wh 2009
2008021051

First Tricycle Press printing, 2009
Printed in China

7 — 19

For my mother, Maria Duarte Tafolla,

for all the *paletas* she gave me,

and for all that she still gives my children.

—C.T.

To my parents, Eligio and Eloína,

whose infinite love is among

the most delicious flavors of life.

I love them with all of my colors!

—M.M.

Where the big velvet roses bloom
red and pink and fuchsia,
where the accordion plays sassy and sweet,

where the smell of crispy tacos
or buttery tortillas
or juicy *fruta*
floats out of every window,

and where the paleta wagon
rings its tinkly bell
and carries a treasure of icy *paletas*
in every color of the *sarape* . . .

THAT'S my *barrio!*

You can dance to the accordion,
you can smell the tacos, but . . .

WHAT can you DO with a *paleta*?

You can paint your tongue purple and green,

and scare your brother!

Or maybe learn to make tough decisions.
Strawberry? Or coconut?

You can make new friends,

give yourself a big, blue mustache,

or create a masterpiece!

You can use one to cool off,
like Mama does!

Tío once won a baseball game
by offering one to the batter
(right when the ball was being pitched!).

You can help the *señora* at the fruit stand
make it through a long, hard day.

But I think the very best thing
to do with a *paleta* is to . . .

lick it and slurp it
and sip it and munch it
and gobble it all down.

Where the big, velvet roses
bloom red and pink and fuchsia,

where the accordion plays sassy and sweet,
where the smell of crispy tacos
or buttery tortillas
or juicy *fruta*
floats out of every window,

and where the *paleta* wagon
rings its tinkly bell
and carries a treasure of icy *paletas*
in every color of the *sarape* . . .

THAT'S my *barrio!*

ABOUT *PALETAS*

A much-anticipated event in any Latino *barrio* ("neighborhood") is the arrival of the *paleta* wagon. The *paleta* man comes pushing his cart down the street, tinkling a bell and shouting, "*Pale-ta-a-a-as!*" for everyone to hear. The wagon carries sweet, juicy, ice-cold *paletas* made from all-natural, healthy ingredients.

Paletas come in lime, coconut, pecan, mango, banana, kiwi, strawberry, watermelon, guava, chocolate, *horchata, jamaica,* tamarind, pineapple, vanilla, and more.

Which is YOUR favorite?

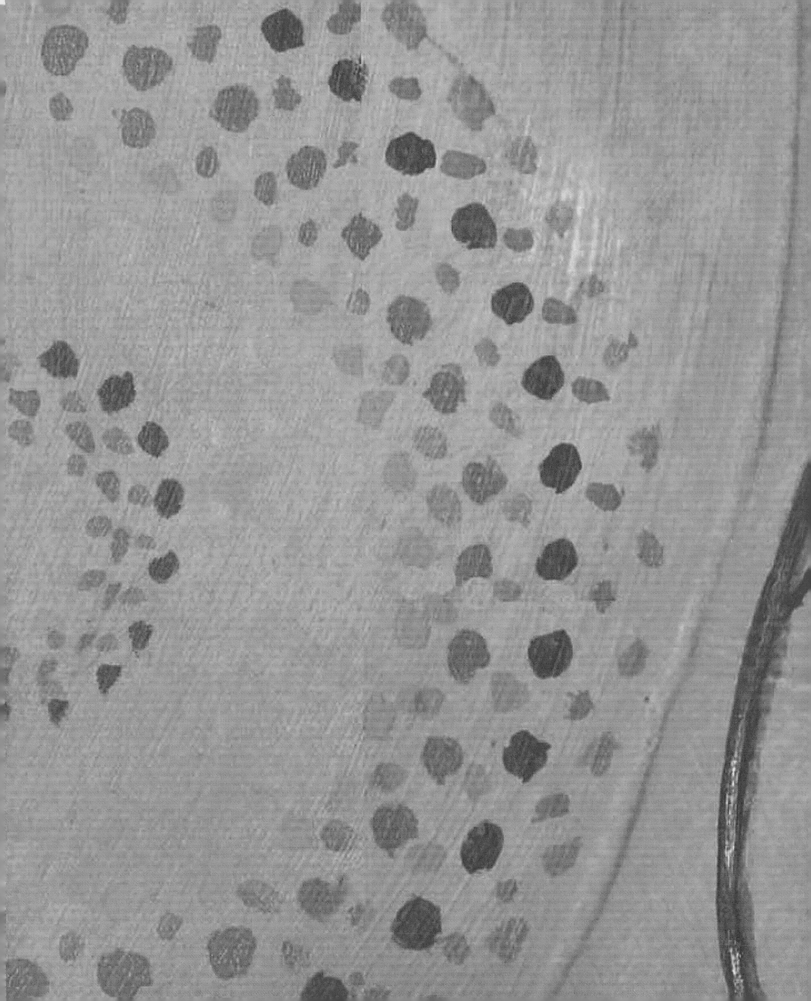

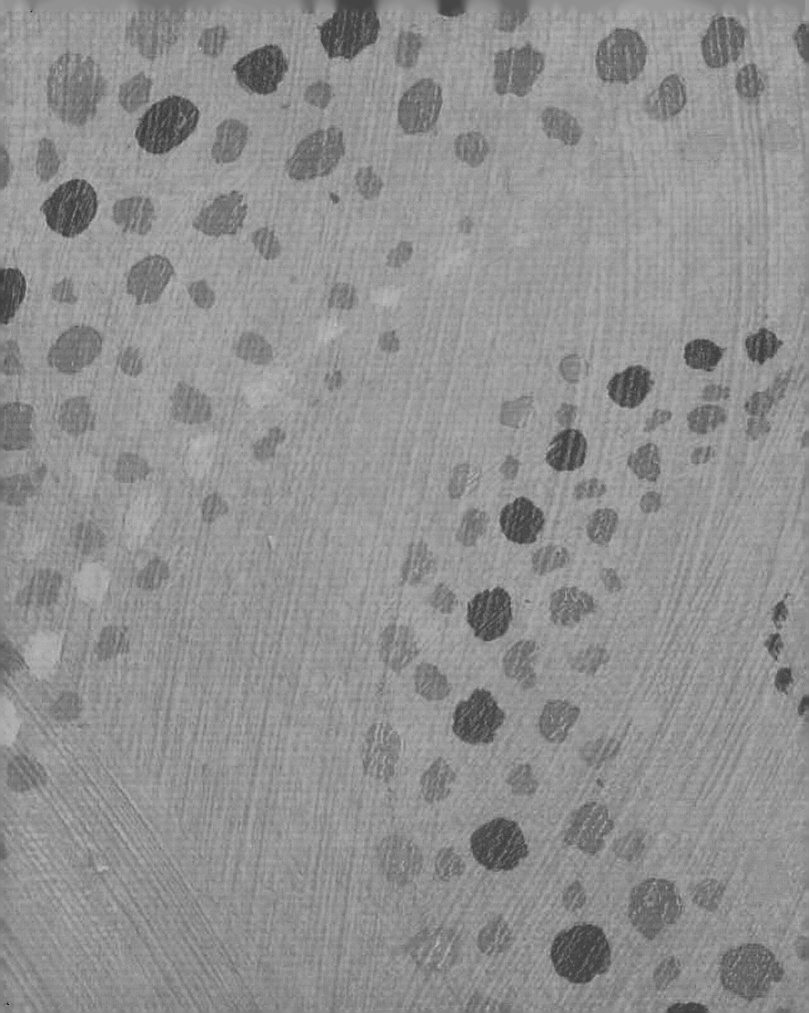